Diable, a Dog

A Jamestown
Classic
adapted from
Jack London

Walter Pauk, Ph.D.
Professor of Education
Director, Reading-Study Center
Cornell University

Raymond Harris

Jamestown
Publishers

Providence
Rhode Island

Diable, a Dog

Student Booklet, No.513

adapted from
Jack London

Cover, Text Design by Stephen R. Anthony
Illustrations by Robert James Pailthorpe

Printed in the United States
79 80 81 82 9 8 7 6 5 4 3 2

ISBN 0-89061-046-0

Contents

Diable, a Dog

The dog was a devil. This was well known all over the Northland. "Hell's spawn" he was called by many men; but his master, Black Leclaire, chose for him the name Diable.

Now Black Leclaire was also a devil, so the two were well matched. The first time they met, Diable was a puppy. He was lean and hungry, and his eyes were mean. They met with a snap and a snarl and evil looks, because Leclaire's lip had a way of lifting and showing his cruel white teeth . . . like a wolf.

He reached for Diable and dragged him out from the litter of pups. The next minute, Diable had sunk his puppy fangs in Leclaire's hand, and he had to choke the dog to make him let go. "Damn!" the Frenchman said softly. He threw the dog into the snow and shook the blood from his hand.

Leclaire turned to John Hamlin, the storekeeper of the Sixty Mile Post, and said, "That's what I like heem for. How much, hey? How much? I buy heem now." And Leclaire bought Diable because he hated him.

They traveled about the wilds of the Yukon country together for five years. Both were well known for their evil and wickedness, the like of which had never been known in a man and dog.

Diable's father was a great gray timber wolf. His mother was a snarling, fighting husky with a wicked eye and a grip on life like a cat. She was a genius at trickery and evil, and she had no faith or trust in man or animal.

There was much evil and much strength in Diable's parents. And bone and flesh of their bone and flesh, he had gotten it all. Then came Black Leclaire to lay his heavy hand on that bit of puppy life, to press it and mold it until it became a big wolf-like beast, clever, hateful, sinister, and evil.

The story of Leclaire and the dog is a story of war—five cruel years of it. They hated each other, but there was a difference. Leclaire hated and knew why he hated. The long-legged puppy hated blindly without reason or method.

At first there was just ordinary cruelty—simple beating and kicking. In one of these beatings, Diable had an ear hurt. He never had control of the torn muscles after that, and the ear drooped. The dog never forgot.

His puppy yelps passed with his lanky legs. He became grim and quiet, quick to strike, slow to warn. He answered curse with snarl, blow with snap—all the while grinning his hatred. And never again, even in the worst agony, did Leclaire bring from him a cry of fear or pain.

Diable became a terror to all dogs and masters of dogs. When Leclaire beat him and petted Babette—Babette who was not half the worker he was—Diable threw her down in the snow and broke her back leg in his jaws so that Leclaire was forced to shoot her. In battle after bloody battle, Diable mastered all his teammates. He set them the law of the trail and made them live to the law he set.

In five years, Diable heard only one kind word, and had one soft stroke of a hand—and then he did not know what they were. He leaped like the untamed thing he was, and his jaws were together in a flash. The hand belonged to the preacher at Sunrise. The doctor from Jimtown had to travel

two hundred miles on the ice to save the unlucky man from blood poisoning.

Once a man kicked Diable. With a quick wolf snap, Diable closed his jaws like a steel trap on the man's leg and bit down to the bone. The man swore he would have the dog's life, but Black Leclaire, with dark eyes and a naked hunting knife, stepped in between.

The killing of Diable—ah, damn! That was a pleasure that Leclaire was saving for himself. Someday it would happen, . . . or else . . . bah! . . . who was to know? Anyhow, one day the problem would be solved.

For they had become problems to each other, this man and beast. The very breath each drew was a threat to the other. Their hate tied them together as love never could. Leclaire had made up his mind he would see the day when Diable would wilt in spirit and crawl at his feet. And Diable—Leclaire knew what was in Diable's mind. More than once he had read it in the dog's eyes. So clearly had he read it, that when the dog was at his back, he was careful to glance often over his shoulder.

Men were surprised that Diable did not run away. They did not understand. But Leclaire understood. Leclaire was a man who had lived in the wilderness all his life—beyond the sound of human voices. He had learned the voices of wind and storm, the whisper of dawn, the clash of day. In a way, he could hear the green things growing. And he knew the speech of things that moved—the rabbit in the snare, the beating of a crow's wings and the wolf gliding like a gray shadow between the light and the dark. And to him Diable spoke clear and direct. He knew why Diable did not run away. And he looked more often over his shoulder.

Diable learned to wait. And when he reached his full strength, he thought the time had come. He was broad chested and powerful. His neck from head to shoulders was a mass of wiry hair. He looked for all the world like a full-blooded wolf.

One night, Leclaire was lying asleep in his furs when Diable decided the time was right. He crept up on the sleeping man, head low to the earth and his one good ear laid back. The dog breathed gently, very gently. Not till he was very close did he raise his head. Then, he stopped for a minute and looked at the strong bull throat of the man—naked and swelling in a deep and steady beat.

The saliva dripped down his fangs and slid off his tongue at the sight, and in that moment he remembered his drooping ear and all the beatings and wrongs put upon him. Without a sound, he sprang.

Leclaire awoke with the pain of fangs in his throat. And perfect animal that he was, he awoke clearheaded and with full understanding of what was happening. He closed on the dog's windpipe with both his hands and rolled out of his furs to get his weight on top.

When Leclaire's weight came on top of him, Diable drove his back legs up and in and clawed down Leclaire's chest and stomach, ripping and tearing through skin and muscle. Then, feeling the body above him move with the pain, he shook and tore at the man's throat.

The other dogs of the team closed around in a snarling circle. Diable knew that their jaws were hungry for him, but that did not matter. It was the man—the man above him—and he ripped and shook and clawed to the last ounce of his strength.

But Leclaire choked him with both his hands till Diable's chest cried for air and his eyes glazed and his jaws slowly loosened and his tongue hung out black and swollen.

"Hey, good, you devil!" Leclaire gurgled, his mouth and throat clogged with his own blood. Then he cursed and kicked the other dogs off as they fell on Diable for the kill.

Diable recovered quickly, and at the sound of Leclaire's voice, rose weakly to his feet.

"Ah-hah you beeg devil!" Leclaire screamed. "I feex you. I feex you plenty by Gar!"

With the air biting into his gasping lungs like sweet wine, Diable flashed full into the man's face, his jaws missing and coming together with a snap. The two of them rolled over and over on the snow, Leclaire striking madly with his fists.

Then they separated, face to face, and circled back and forth before each other for an opening. Leclaire could have drawn his knife. His rifle was at his feet. But the beast in him was up and raging. He would do the thing with his hands—and his teeth.

The dog sprang in, but Leclaire knocked him over with a blow of his fist, fell on him and buried his teeth to the bone in the dog's shoulder. It was a scene that might have been seen in the savage youth of the world. An open space in a dark forest. A ring of grinning wolf dogs. And in the center, two beasts, locked in combat, snapping and snarling, ripping and tearing and clawing in a fury of murder.

Finally Leclaire hit the dog behind the ear with a blow from his fist, knocking him over. He leaped on the beast with both feet and jumped up and down, trying to grind him into the earth. Before Leclaire stopped to catch a breath, both of Diable's hind legs were broken.

"A-a-ah! A-a-ah!" Leclaire screamed, unable to talk.

Diable lay in a horrible, helpless heap. And still his lip lifted in a feeble snarl. Leclaire kicked him, and the tired jaws closed on the ankle, but could not break the skin.

Then Leclaire picked up the whip and began to almost cut him to pieces. With each stroke of the lash he cried: "Thees time I break you! Eh? By Gar, I break you!"

In the end, tired and fainting from loss of blood, Leclaire fell by his victim. And when the wolf dogs closed in to take their revenge, with his last ounce of strength, Leclaire dragged his body on top of Diable to save him from the circle of fangs.

This happened not far from Sunrise, and the preacher, opening his door to Leclaire a few hours later, was surprised that Diable was missing from the team. He was even more surprised when Leclaire threw back the robes from the sled, took Diable into his arms, and carried him inside to the fire. By chance, the doctor from Jimtown was up for a visit, and between them they began to patch up Leclaire.

"No . . . thank you, please," Leclaire said. "You feex first the dog. To die? No. It is not good. Because heem I must yet break. That's for what he must not die."

The doctor called it a wonder and the preacher called it a miracle that Leclaire lived through it all. But he was so weak that in the Spring the fever got him and he went on his back again. The dog had been even worse, but his grip on life was strong. Soon the bones in his back legs mended, his insides came right again, and by the time Leclaire was able to take some sun by the cabin door, Diable had already regained command of the team and of the preacher's dogs as well. He never moved a muscle or a hair when Leclaire came out of the cabin for the first time, leaning on the preacher's arm.

"Good!" he said. "Good! The good sun!" And he held out his hands and washed them in the warm sunshine.

Then he saw the dog, and the old light blazed back in his eyes. He touched the preacher's arm. "My Father, that is one beeg devil, that Diable. You will bring me a pistol so that I can drink the sun in peace, yes?"

And so for many days he sat in the sun before the cabin door. The pistol was always on his knees. The dog had a way, first thing in the morning, of looking for the gun. When he saw it, he would lift his lip in an easy snarl as a sign that he understood. And Leclaire would lift his own lip in an answering grin.

One day the preacher watched this in amazement. "Bless me!" he said. "I really believe the animal understands."

Leclaire laughed softly. "Look you, my Father. That what I now speak, to that does he listen."

Diable wiggled his one good ear to catch the sound.

"I say . . . kill . . . ."

Diable growled deep down in his throat. The hair stood up along his neck and every muscle went tense—waiting.

"I lift the gun, so, like that . . . ." And Leclaire pointed the pistol at the dog.

With a single leap, Diable jumped sideways, landing around the corner of the cabin, out of sight.

"Why, bless me!" the preacher said. "Bless me!"

Leclaire grinned proudly.

"But why doesn't he run away?"

Leclaire shrugged his shoulders.

"Then why don't you kill him?"

Leclaire shrugged again.

"My Father," he said after a while, "the time is not yet. He is one beeg devil. Some time I break heem, so and so—all to little bits. Eh? Some time. Good!"

For two years after that, Leclaire wandered through the Yukon country, first on a job for the P.C. Company and then exploring and then prospecting for gold. Diable stayed with him and suffered all the tortures the man could think of for him.

But all bad things come to an end as well as good things, and so with Black Leclaire. One summer, in a canoe, he left the town of Pelly for Sunrise. He left Pelly with Timothy Brown, and arrived at Sunrise by himself.

It was known that Leclaire and Brown had fought just before pulling out. And when Leclaire got to Sunrise, it was with a bullet hole in his shoulder and a story of ambush and murder.

A gold strike had been made at Sunrise, and things had changed there. Hundreds of gold seekers, a good deal of raw whiskey and about a dozen gamblers had come to town. And the preacher had seen all his years of labor with the Indians wiped clean.

The squaws were cooking beans and keeping the fire going all night for the wifeless miners, and the braves were swapping their warm furs for black bottles of booze. So the preacher

took to his bed, said "Bless me!" several times, and went to his final rest in a rough wooden box.

After that, the gamblers moved their dice and black-jack tables into the mission house, and the click of chips and clink of glasses went up from dawn till dark and to dawn again.

Now Timothy Brown was well loved among these men of the north. The one thing against him was his quick temper and ready fists. But these were little things, which his big heart more than made up for. On the other hand, there was nothing that made up for Black Leclaire. He was as well hated as Brown was well loved. So the men of Sunrise put a bandage on Leclaire's shoulder and brought him to see Judge Lynch.

It was all so simple. He had fought with Timothy Brown at Pelly. *With* Timothy Brown he had left Pelly. *Without* Timothy Brown he had arrived at Sunrise. So when thought of in the light of his evilness, everyone decided that Leclaire had killed Timothy Brown.

However, Leclaire said that twenty miles out of Sunrise, he and Timothy Brown were paddling along the rocky shore. Two rifle shots rang out. Timothy Brown fell out of the canoe and went down in a pool of red, and that was the last of Timothy Brown. He, Leclaire, fell to the bottom of the canoe with a bullet in his shoulder.

After a time, two Indians stuck their heads up and came out to the water's edge. When they did that, Leclaire let fly. He potted one, who fell into the river, and the other ran. That was all.

This story was not enough to make up for the loss of Timothy Brown, so they gave Leclaire ten hours to live while they steamed down the river in the paddle boat *Lizzie* to look things over.

No proof was found to back up Leclaire's story. So they told him to make a will, because he owned a $50,000 gold claim in Sunrise, and they were a law-abiding as well as a law-giving breed of men.

Leclaire shrugged his shoulders. He had faced death too many times before to let it bother him now. "But one thing," he said. "What you call a little favor. A little favor, that is it. I give my $50,000 to the church. I give my husky dog Diable to the devil. The little favor? First you hang him . . . and then you hang me. It is good, eh?"

Good it was, they agreed. That Hell's Spawn should break trail for his master across the last divide. Judge, jury, audience and prisoner went to the riverbank where a big spruce tree stood by itself. Slackwater Charley put a hangman's knot in the end of a rope and the noose was slipped over Leclaire's head and pulled tight around his neck.

His hands were tied behind his back and he was helped to the top of a cracker box. The other end of the rope was passed over a branch of the spruce tree, drawn tight and made fast. To kick the box out from under Leclaire was all that was left to do.

"Now for the dog," said Webster Shaw. "You'll have to rope him Slackwater."

Leclaire grinned. Slackwater took a chew of tobacco, made a lasso and coiled a few turns in his hand. Diable was lying stretched on the ground watching his master with interest.

But while Slackwater was waiting for Diable to lift his head so he could get the rope over him, a faint call came across the quiet air. A man was seen waving his arm and running across the flat from Sunrise. It was the storekeeper.

"Call it off boys," he panted as he ran in among them. "Little Sandy and Big Bernard just got in. They landed down below and came up the short cut. They got Big Beaver with them. He's got two bullet holes in him, and they left his buddy Klok-Kutz at the bottom of the river, twenty miles down stream."

"Eh? What I tell you? Eh?" Leclaire cried. "That the one for sure! I know. I speak true—you see?"

"The thing to do then," spoke Webster Shaw, "is to string up the Beaver for an object lesson. That's the program. Come on and let's see what he's got to say for himself."

"Hey, mister!" Leclaire called as the crowd began to melt away in the direction of Sunrise. "I like very much to come down from this cracker box and see the fun."

"Oh, we'll turn you loose when we get back," Webster Shaw shouted over his shoulder. "In the meantime, you think about your sins. It will do you good, so be thankful."

As is the way with men who are used to danger, and whose nerves are healthy and trained to stay calm, Leclaire settled himself to the long wait. That is, he settled his mind to it, because the tight rope forced him to stand stiff and straight— almost on tiptoe. The least easing of his leg muscles pressed the noose into his neck, while the stiff upright position caused him much pain in his wounded shoulder.

While he was standing thus and thinking, his eyes happened to fall on Diable, head between paws and stretched out on the ground asleep. Then Leclaire stopped his idle thinking. He studied the animal closely trying to sense if the sleep was real or not.

The dog's sides were heaving regularly, but Leclaire felt that the breath came and went a shade too quickly. He also felt that there was an alertness to every hair on the animal. He would have given his Sunrise claim to be sure the dog was not awake. And once when one of his joints cracked, he looked quickly to see if the dog heard.

Diable did not move then, but a few minutes later he got up slowly and lazily, stretched, and looked carefully about him.

"Damn!" said Leclaire under his breath.

When he was sure that no one was in sight or hearing, Diable sat down, curled his upper lip almost into a smile, looked up at Leclaire and licked his chops.

"Ah . . . so here I see my finish," the man said, and laughed out loud.

Diable came nearer, his dead ear wobbling, the good one cocked forward with devilish understanding. He set his head on one side and came forward with little playful steps. He rubbed his body against the cracker box till it shook and shook again.

"Diable," Leclaire said calmly, "you look out, 'cause I kill you."

Diable snarled at the word and shook the box even harder. Then he reared up and threw his weight against the box higher up with his front paws. Leclaire kicked out with one foot, but the rope bit into his neck and he almost fell off his perch.

"Hi! Yah! Mush on!" he screamed.

Diable backed off twenty feet or so with a fiendish joy which Leclaire could not mistake. He remembered how the dog could break the scum of ice from a water hole by lifting up and throwing his weight on it. And remembering, he understood what the dog had in mind. Diable faced around and paused. He showed his white teeth in a grin, which Leclaire answered. And then he hurled his body through the air straight for the box.

Fifteen minutes later, Slackwater Charley and Webster Shaw returned to find a ghostly plaything swinging from the spruce tree. As they hurried closer, they made out Leclaire's body and a live thing that was hanging to it, shaking it and growling and trying to pull it down.

"Hi! Yah! Chook! you Spawn of Hell!" Webster Shaw yelled.

Diable glared at him and snarled without letting go of the body. Slackwater Charley got out his pistol, but his hand was shaking so that he couldn't point it.

"Here, you take it," he said, passing the gun to Webster Shaw.

Shaw laughed, drew a sight between the gleaming eyes and pulled the trigger. Diable's body jerked with the shock of the bullet and went limp. But his teeth held fast, locked to the hated body above him.

Glossary

Glossary

Diable, a Dog
A Glossary of Words and Expressions

Key Concepts

Key Concepts

Diable, a Dog
Understanding Key Concepts—Examining Values

These are short passages taken from the story, followed by three questions. In every case, question A can be answered without knowing the story and may be used for warm-up discussions.

Questions B and C should be kept in mind, while listening to the story or reading it, for discussion later. Answers to the A questions may also be reviewed at this time.

1. Black Leclaire is about to buy a puppy to use as a sled dog (page 9):

> He reached for Diable and dragged him out from the litter of pups. The next minute, Diable had sunk his puppy fangs in Leclaire's hand . . . . "Damn!" the Frenchman said softly . . . . "That's what I like heem for. How much, hey?" . . . . And Leclaire bought Diable because he hated him.

A. What would be your reasons for buying a dog—as a pet, or as a working dog?

B. Explain the feelings between Leclaire and Diable.

C. Find a passage in the story that tries to explain why Leclaire and Diable stayed together.

2. We are told that Leclaire used to beat Diable (page 10):

> At first there was just ordinary cruelty—simple beating and kicking. In one of these beatings, Diable had an ear hurt . . . . The dog never forgot.

A. What is your opinion of beatings or other forms of punishment as a way to train a person or an animal?

B. Some people think that Leclaire and Diable deserved each other. What do you think?

C. Would you say that one moral of the story is: "Revenge is sweet"?

3. Describing a fight to the death between Leclaire and his dog Diable, the author says (page 13):

> Leclaire could have drawn his knife. His rifle was at his feet. But the beast in him was up and raging. He would do the thing with his hands—and his teeth.

A. If you owned a vicious dog that attacked you, what would you do?

B. What possible reasons could a man have for using his hands and teeth against a vicious dog when he could have used a knife or gun?

C. Whom did you want to win the fight? Explain your feelings. Do you think the story would have been better if it had ended here, with Diable winning?

4. Continuing the description of the death struggle between Leclaire and his dog Diable, the author tells us (page 13):

> It was a scene that might have been seen in the savage youth of the world. An open space in a dark forest . . . . And in the center, two beasts, locked in combat, snapping and snarling . . . .

A. The author is calling the man, Leclaire, a beast. In what ways can people be like beasts? Humans *are* animals, of course. But what are the *important* differences between dogs and people?

B. There is much to dislike about both Leclaire and Diable. What did you *like* about them?

C. Do you think the people of Sunrise were better human beings than Leclaire? Explain your opinion.

5. The dog Diable would look to see if Leclaire had a pistol in his lap. If he did, Diable would snarl and Leclaire would snarl back. Watching this, a preacher said (page 15):

> "Bless me! . . . I really believe the animal understands."

A. Can dogs understand things the way you do?

B. What parts of the story lead you to believe that Diable could think and feel like a man?

C. In your opinion, did the author make Leclaire too much like an animal and Diable too much like a man? Why did the author do this anyhow?

Comprehension Questions

Comprehension Questions

Diable, a Dog
How Well Did You Understand the Story?

Choose the letter which best answers each question.

1. The first time Leclaire picked up Diable, the dog
   a. bit him.
   b. licked his hand.
   c. cried.
   d. barked.

2. Leclaire bought Diable because he
   a. loved the dog.
   b. wanted him for a friend.
   c. wanted to help the dog.
   d. hated the dog.

3. Diable went through life with a floppy ear as a result of
   a. a fight with another dog.
   b. a beating from Leclaire.
   c. an accident.
   d. a gunshot wound.

4. Leclaire made up his mind that he would
   a. kill Diable.
   b. beat the dog to death.
   c. break the dog's spirit.
   d. make Diable the lead dog of his team.

5. Diable wanted
   a. to teach Leclaire a lesson.
   b. to break Leclaire's spirit.
   c. to kill Leclaire.
   d. to be free.

6. After their battle, Leclaire
    a. protected Diable from the other dogs.
    b. let the other dogs get even with Diable.
    c. shot Diable.
    d. stabbed the dog with his knife.

7. The people of Sunrise accused Leclaire of
    a. horse stealing.
    b. killing Timothy Brown.
    c. cruelty to Diable.
    d. killing an Indian.

8. It turned out that Leclaire was
    a. guilty.
    b. innocent.
    c. innocent because Diable was guilty.
    d. guilty and Diable had helped him.

9. Leclaire's end came when Diable
    a. helped Timothy Brown in his fight with Leclaire.
    b. broke a hole through the ice and Leclaire drowned.
    c. led the people of Sunrise to where Leclaire was hiding.
    d. pushed a cracker box out from under Leclaire and hanged him.

10. When Webster Shaw and Slackwater Charlie returned to find Leclaire dead, they
    a. petted Diable.
    b. shot Diable.
    c. freed Diable.
    d. chased Diable.

Discussion Starters

Discussion Starters

Diable, a Dog
Discussion Starters

1. Was Diable born mean? Was Diable mean because his parents were mean? Did Leclaire make Diable mean? Do you know any mean people? Are some people born mean or do they become that way because of the way life treats them?

2. The author, Jack London, tells us that Leclaire and Diable hated each other. But he said there was a difference in the way each hated. Can hates be different or is all hate the same? In what way did the author think Leclaire's hate was different from Diable's? What is hate?

3. Would you say that when Diable grew up he became like Leclaire? What was animal-like about Leclaire? What was human about Leclaire? What do you think the author was trying to say about some animals and some humans?

4. Diable would not run away. Would you have run away from Leclaire? Leclaire was careful not to kill Diable. If you were Leclaire, would you have killed the dog? Why do some people mistreat animals?

5. Was the fight between Leclaire and Diable a fair one since Leclaire would not use his gun or knife? Do you approve of fights to the death as long as they are fair? What is your opinion of fighting?

6. Did Leclaire ever "break" Diable? Did Diable "break" Leclaire? Was there a "winner" in the story?

7. What do you think of the system of justice in the town of Sunrise? Do you think that the way they did things was funny? Is our modern system of justice better?

8. Did the story turn out "right" in the end? Was justice done when Diable was shot? How important is justice and fairness?

9. Did Diable get even with Leclaire? How important is getting even in life?

10. Diable was unable to kill Leclaire by fighting nature's way with bare teeth and claws. But Diable *was* able to kill Leclaire in a "civilized" way by hanging him. What do you think the author is trying to say to the reader by describing such a situation?